The Little Wood Duck

FOR ANNA

OXFORD
UNIVERSITY PRESS

Great Clarendon Street, Oxford OX2 6DP

Oxford University Press is a department of the University of Oxford.
It furthers the University's objective of excellence in research, scholarship,
and education by publishing worldwide in

Oxford New York

Athens Auckland Bangkok Bogotá Buenos Aires Calcutta
Cape Town Chennai Dar es Salaam Delhi Florence Hong Kong Istanbul
Karachi Kuala Lumpur Madrid Melbourne Mexico City Mumbai
Nairobi Paris São Paulo Singapore Taipei Tokyo Toronto Warsaw

with associated companies in Berlin Ibadan

Oxford is a registered trade mark of Oxford University Press
in the UK and in certain other countries

ISBN 0-19-272401-0

Printed in Hong Kong

BRIAN WILDSMITH

The Little Wood Duck

OXFORD
UNIVERSITY PRESS

Once upon a time, in an old tree, beside a lake, a mother Wood Duck built her nest. And in the nest she laid six beautiful eggs. "Come and see," she quacked. "I'm so excited. I've laid such a lot of eggs. I have never laid so many before."

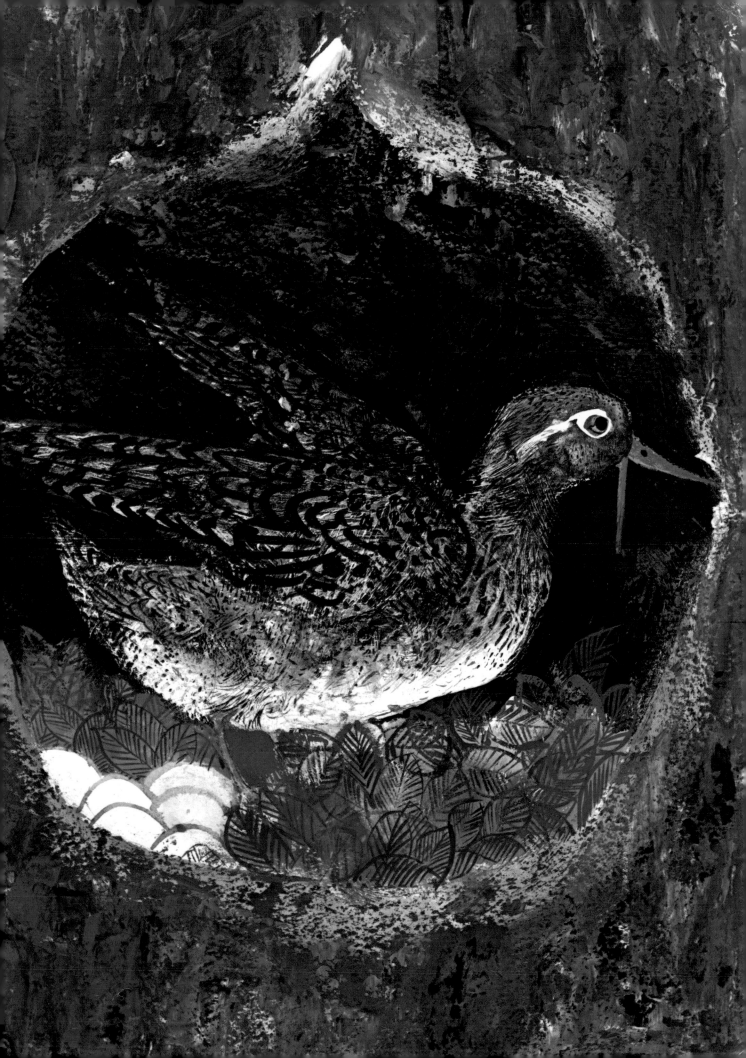

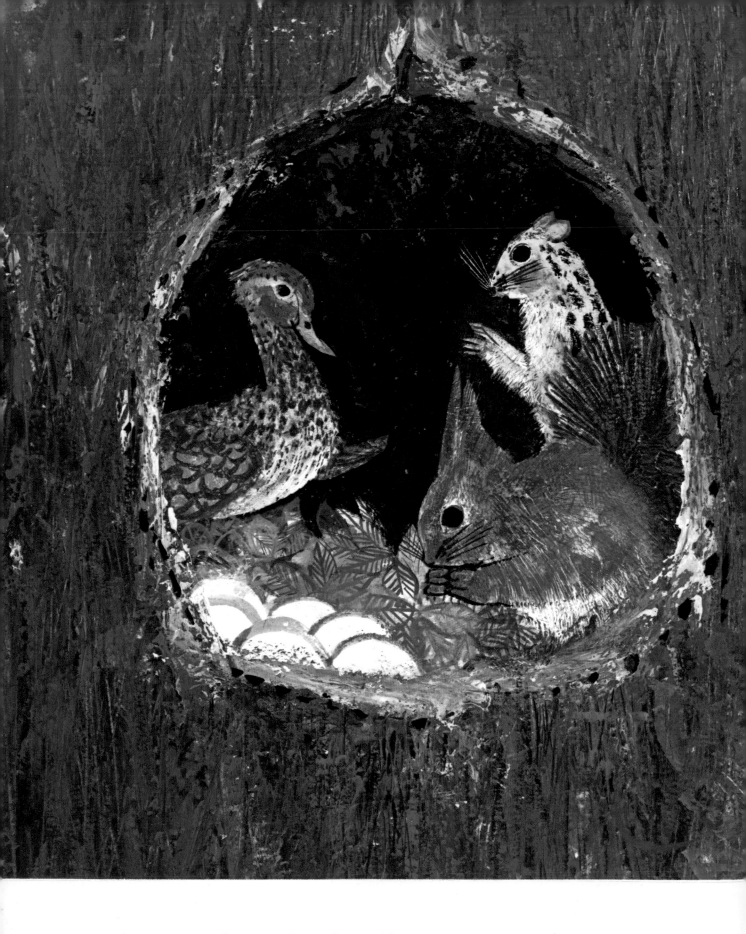

The Wood Duck's friends came hurrying to see the eggs. They were nearly as excited as the mother duck herself.

"Soon I shall have six handsome ducklings," boasted
the Wood Duck, as she settled her feathers over the
eggs to keep them warm.

Day after day the Wood Duck sat
patiently on her eggs. But she could

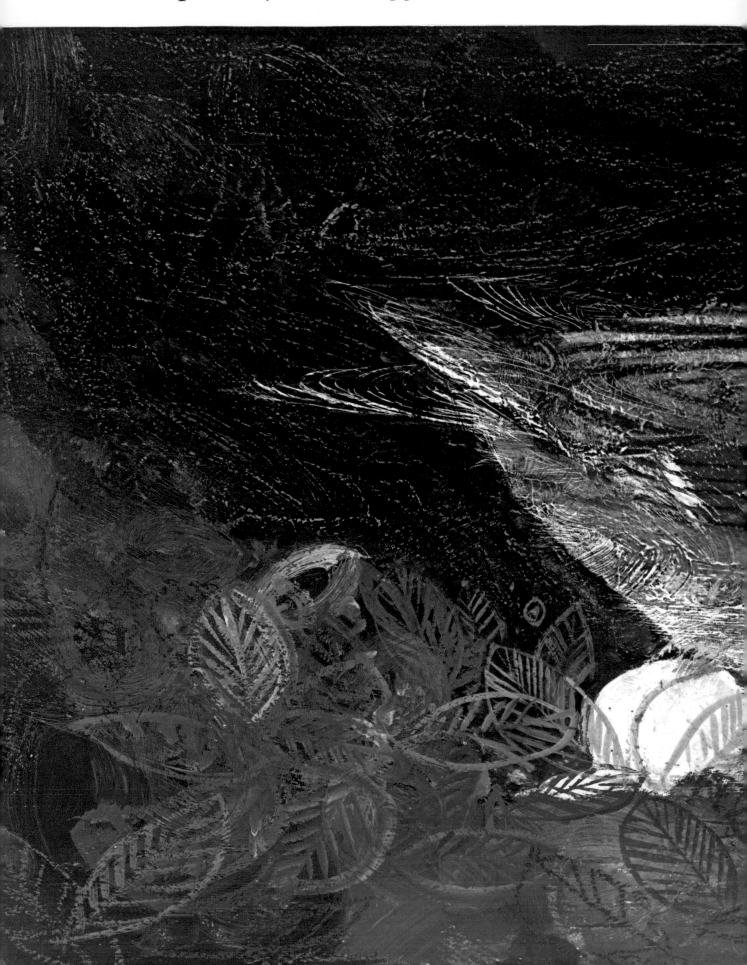

not resist taking a peep now and then
to see if one of them had hatched.

At last the little ducklings broke out of the eggs, and were soon chasing each other around the tree.

The Wood Duck watched over them with pride. She longed for them to be big enough to take their first swim in the lake.

Then, one warm, clear day the mother duck called her children to her, and took them down to the water's edge.

Without a moment's hesitation the ducklings jumped into the water, and swam in a nice straight line in and out of the reeds.
All except one! The youngest duckling swam all by

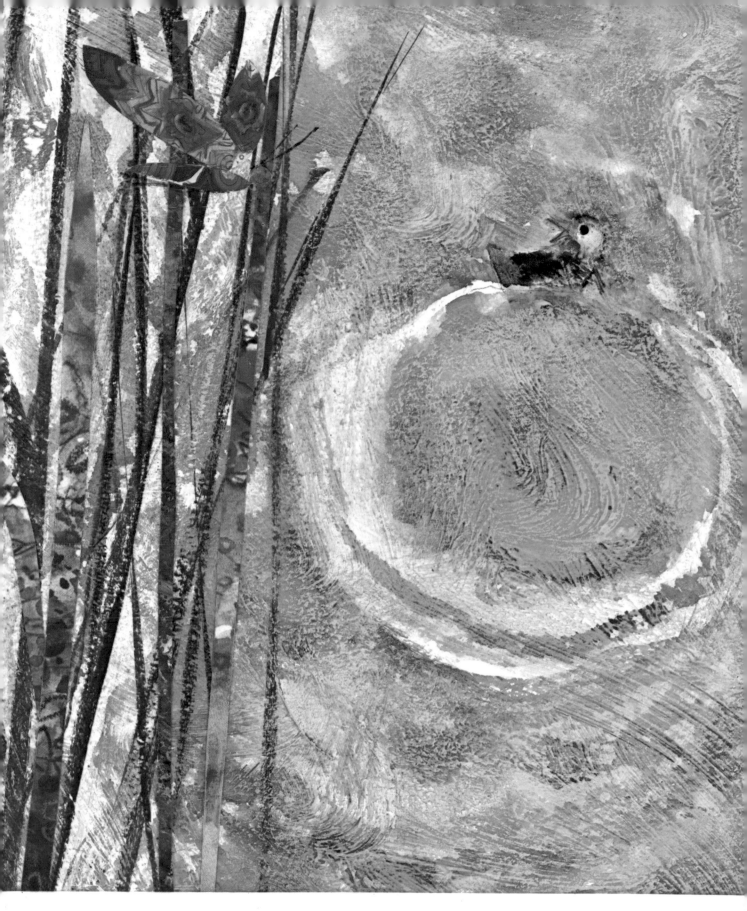

himself – round and round, in a circle.
The other ducklings called to him to play with them
in the reeds, but the youngest Wood Duck just went
on swimming round and round.

Every day the ducklings followed their mother to the water, and practised their swimming. But the youngest duckling always swam by himself, and he always swam in circles.

"He just doesn't want to swim with us," complained his five brothers and sisters.

"Come here at once," the mother duck cried angrily. "It is very silly to keep swimming round and round like that."

"But I can't do it any other way," wailed the youngest Wood Duck.

"That's nonsense," said the mother duck.

But no matter what his mother said the youngest duckling went on swimming in circles. His mother became angry, his brothers and sisters poked fun at him, and the little Wood Duck felt very unhappy.

"I do try," he said to himself. "But I just can't swim any other way."

The other animals began to tease him.
"Silly old roundabout," shouted the Moose.

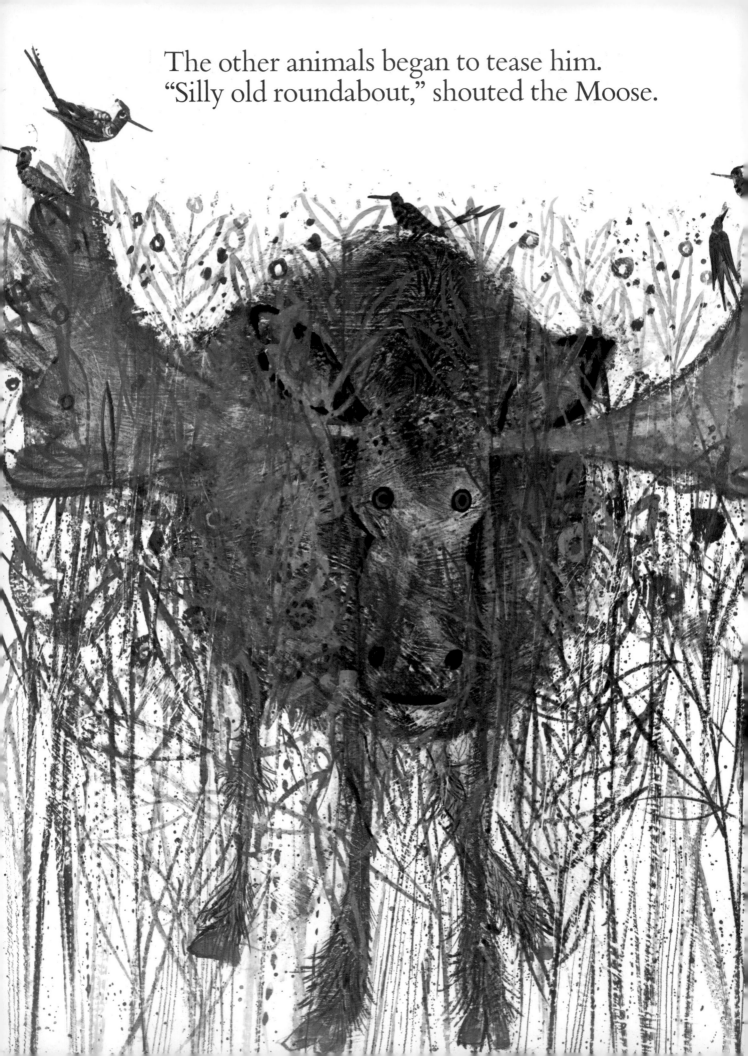

"I bet you can't even see straight," growled the Bear.

The other animals who were watching
from the bank laughed unkindly.
The little Wood Duck grew more and more unhappy.

Then one day, an owl who was flying past heard the teasing and swooped down to see what was going on.

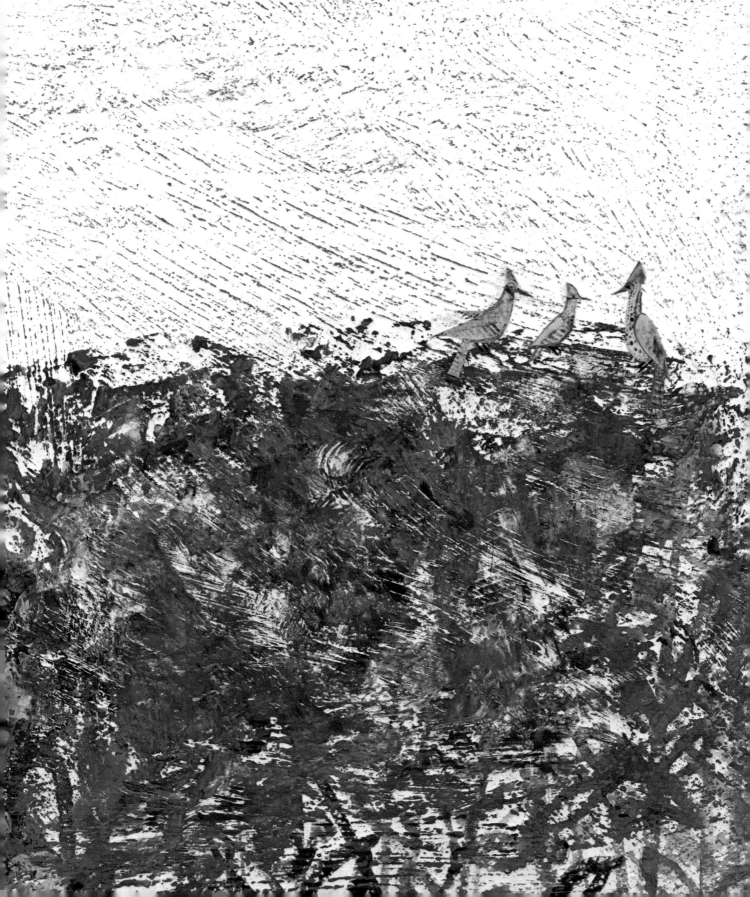

He called the duckling out of the water, and asked him to tell him his troubles. While the little Wood Duck explained about his swimming the owl looked him over carefully.

"Why, young fellow," cried the owl. "You have one foot larger than the other. That is why you go round and round. But never mind, there is nothing wrong in swimming in circles. Take no notice of these silly animals."

And the owl scolded the other animals for being so stupid and unkind.

About a week later a hungry fox came to the lakeside,
and stood waiting for the ducklings to come ashore.

But the five brothers and sisters hid among the reeds, shaking with fright.
Only the youngest Wood Duck kept on swimming. Round and round he went, while the fox settled down to watch and wait.

But all at once the fox felt rather strange. He had watched the duckling swimming round and round for so long that he began to feel dizzy. He felt that not

only the duckling was going round and round, but the grass and the trees and the sky and the lake as well.

"Oh dear!" gasped the fox, and fell flat on his back, too giddy even to sit.

At once all the little ducklings raced for the shore and home to their mother.

They all tried to tell her the story at once – except for the youngest duckling who stood modestly by. But his mother was proud of him, and all his brothers and sisters crowded round to cheer. "We will never tease you again," they said. And they never did, for the little Wood Duck was a hero now, and everybody admired his wonderful circles, and the tremendous speed of his swimming